TO MY UNCLE AND MY FAVOURITE
LITTLE ARTISTS: SÓLEY, ABRIL, JOAN,
CARLES AND MILA. ☺

First published 2013 by Macmillan Children's Books
a division of Macmillan Publishers Limited
20 New Wharf Road, London N1 9RR
Basingstoke and Oxford
Associated companies throughout the world
www.panmacmillan.com

ISBN: 978-0-230-76040-0 (HB)

Text and illustrations copyright © Marta Altés 2013
Moral rights asserted.

5 7 9 8 6

A CIP catalogue record for this book is available
from the British Library.

Printed in Belgium.

I AM AN ARTIST

marta altés

MACMILLAN CHILDREN'S BOOKS

I am an artist.

So is my mum!

But in a VERY different way.

Everywhere I look, I see ART.

But I don't think my mum always sees it.

Where I see *The Loneliness of the Carrot,*

my mum sees *An Unfinished Dinner.*

Where I see *A Window to the World,*

my mum sees *A Hole in the Wall.*

(I don't think she understands me.)

But I CAN'T STOP CREATING!
Some of my finest pieces of art this week are:

Blue Number 10,

Blue Number 11,

and *Blue Number 12.*

This one is my *Multiple Self Portrait*.

And I think I'll call this one,
Spring in Winter.

I am SO talented,
I just can't help it.

EVERYTHING

inspires me!

I love NATURE

COLOURS

MOVEMENT

TEXTURES

and SHAPES

But there's just one problem . . .

my mum.

I think maybe something is wrong.
Perhaps I haven't given her enough attention.

There must be something I can do
to make her feel better . . .

mmmmmmmmmm . . .

I KNOW!!

I am going to make an AMAZING
piece of art, especially for her.

But it will need plenty of careful planning.

I can't wait for her to wake up.

I hope she likes it!

I call it,
Ode to My Mum.